THE ANAGRANIMALS AND THE WISHING TREE

(First Edition)

www.Anagranimals.com

First published in 2013 by Anagranimals Ltd
www.Anagranimals.com

Printed in the United Kingdom.
A CIP record of this book is available from the British Library.
ISBN 978-0-9926049-0-5

THE ANAGRANIMALS AND THE WISHING TREE

Leith Moghli

ILLUSTRATED BY
IAN KING

Far, far away, beyond the mountains and across the sea, on the banks of a mighty lake and shrouded in trees, lies a mysterious land called Pogo Bogo.

The hot, steamy forests and green grassy plains of Pogo Bogo are home to every kind of animal that you could imagine.
There are lions and lemurs, tigers and tapirs, elephants and emus, rhinos and reindeers, giraffes, hippos, crocodiles, zebras and even the occasional kangaroo.

Of all the many weird and wonderful creatures on Pogo Bogo, six animals in particular are especially famous. Every beast worth its pelt has heard of George the Giraffe, Pedro the Pig, Heidi the Hippo, Rocky the Rhino, Ebenezer the Elephant and Lancelot the Lion.

The gang's fame is due partly to the fact that their mischievous antics are the stuff of legend but is mainly because of a very magical and marvellous thing that happened to them one day...

As with every good story, it all started with a game of hide and seek. Pedro the Pig was hiding in the long grass. Unfortunately, Pedro was never very good at hide and seek. He made so much noise oinking and clattering around that the rest of the gang quickly knew where to find him. The gang crept slowly towards Pedro's hiding place.

"He must be around here somewhere," yelled Heidi the Hippo playfully, "I can smell him."

The other animals all sniggered. Then, Ebenezer the Elephant said in a low, scary voice "Pedro Pig...., I am the monster of Pogo Bogo.... and I'm coming to get you."

Again, the other animals sniggered. Pedro's face was buried in the long grass so he didn't see Rocky the Rhino creeping up behind him. Rocky grabbed Pedro's piggy tail and shouted at the top of his voice

......"Booo – got you!!!"

Pedro leapt into the air with a big squeak and started running as fast as his piggy legs would carry him. The rest of the gang bounded after Pedro shrieking and laughing as they ran. All of a sudden, in a puff of dust and flying grass, the gang found themselves falling down a steep slope with Pedro tumbling out in front.

They rolled down the slope, horns, trunks and heads over heels until they came to a sudden stop against a thick tree trunk.

"Who goes there?" boomed a thunderous voice.

The gang scrambled to their feet and looked around in astonishment.

"Who said that?" whispered Heidi.

"I did!" replied the voice even louder.

"Who are you?" asked Heidi nervously.

"I am the Wishing Tree," responded the voice.

"The Wishing Tree, what's that?" squeaked Pedro.

"Not what, but who," said the Wishing Tree. "I am the Wishing Tree and I am as old as Pogo Bogo itself. My job is to grant any animal that lands at my feet one special wish."

"Really!!" exclaimed George the Giraffe craning his long neck forwards. "You mean we can wish for absolutely anything and you will make it come true?"

"Well, not absolutely anything," replied the Wishing Tree. "I can't turn things into gold because I'm made of wood and the smelting process really toggles my twigs but I can do pretty much anything else."

The gang looked at one another and then at the Wishing Tree.

The Wishing Tree was a great old oak with a thick trunk as wide as a house and long branches that were knotted and gnarled like a goblin's bottom.

"What do you think we should wish for?" asked Lancelot the Lion.

"Why don't we wish for a humungous mountain of jelly and ice cream?" said Pedro licking his lips. "I looove jelly and ice cream!"

"That's a silly wish," said Lancelot. "You would gobble it up in ten minutes flat and give yourself tummy ache. We only get one wish so it needs to be a really good one."

"I know," said Ebenezer, "why don't we wish for the best bits of our favourite animals? Rocky has always wanted to be able to fly like a bird and I would love to be able to gallop like a zebra."

"Ooh ooh, that's a great idea," said George excitedly. "How do we make a wish?"

"You must say your wish silently in your head," explained the Wishing Tree in his low rumbling voice, "and when you wake up in the morning your wish will be granted."

The animals were silent for a long time as they each thought about what they would wish for. When they had made their wishes the gang skipped off home as fast as they could and went straight to bed without any tea. They couldn't wait for the morning to see if their wishes would come true.

Rocky was the first to wake. He did a big stretch like he does every morning. When he looked in the mirror and saw his reflection he screamed,

"Arrggggggh!!!!"

Then the memory of the gang's encounter with the Wishing Tree came flooding back. He looked in the mirror again, this time more closely. Overnight he had grown a pair of fluffy parrot wings. They were a beautiful mixture of red, blue, emerald green and yellow. He looked down at his legs and saw that they were bright green, his feet were a deep shade of orange and he had big suckers at the end of each of his toes.

"Yippee!!" shouted Rocky as he hopped up and down on his new frog legs and flapped his fluffy parrot wings. "My wish has come true. I'm a Rhino- Parra- Rog!!!"

Rocky hopped out of the house and leapt into the air. He spread his wings, flapped them twice and soared high above the trees.

"WEEEEEEE, I'm flying," shouted Rocky.

Rocky did a quick loop the loop and glided towards the lake. When he looked down he could see the rest of the gang coming over the hill. Sure enough, each of them was sporting a funny new body.

Pedro had been transformed into a Pig-Orilla-Roo. He had the same piggy face but had developed big, bulging muscles like a gorilla and was bouncing along on a huge pair of kangaroo feet.

Ebenezer had turned into an Ele-Zeb-Zee. His big elephant head complete with big floppy elephant ears and long elephant trunk was resting on a black and white zebra body and he had grown feet like a chimpanzee with incy wincey chimpanzee toes.

George had taken the form of a Gir-Osti-Duck. His long giraffe neck was still there but he had sprouted a new ostrich body with black and white ostrich feathers and a set of bright orange duck flippers.

Heidi had become a Hippo-Croco-Puss. She had her own pretty pink hippo head, green crocodile scales and a pair of white pussy cat paws.

Lancelot had swapped his old limbs for the body of a Leo-Tiga-Mur. His lion head still looked very splendid with its red-brown mane but now he had a white and orange tiger body and the bottom half of a lemur with little lemur feet and a fluffy black and white lemur tail.

The gang spent the day trying out their new bodies.

Rocky flew with his new wings and hopped around on his frogs legs. Heidi swam in the lake with her crocodile scales and bounded around with her pussy cat paws. Lancelot used his tiger camouflage to creep up and surprise all the other animals and swung through the trees with his lemur tail. Ebenezer galloped and galloped with his zebra legs until he was all puffed out. George waddled around on his duck flippers and Pedro bounced about on his kangaroo feet. They all had so much fun. It was the best day ever!

The next day the gang decided to visit the Wishing Tree to tell him all about the fun they were having with their funny new bodies.

"Hello, Mr Wishing Tree," said Heidi. "We've come to tell you how much we love our funny new bodies. We've been having so much fun swimming and flying and bouncing around. It's been great!"

"Hah Hah," chuckled the Wishing Tree, "I'm very pleased you like them."

"Is there anything that we can do to repay you?" asked Lancelot.

"Hmm, come to think of it, there is something that I could use a little help with," replied the Wishing Tree.

"You name it!" roared Rocky. "What would you like us to do?"

"Well, my cousin, the Weeping Willow is a bit poorly," explained the Wishing Tree, "he's all bunged up and can't weep anymore.
I would like you to take him some magic sap that I have conjured from the berries of the Boo Hoo Bush. Drinking the magic sap will unbung his trunk and clear out his shoots so that he can weep again."

"Easy peasy Ele-Zeb-Zee," said Rocky. "Consider it done."

"It might sound easy," said the Wishing Tree, "but, be warned, the Weeping Willow lives deep in the Serpent Mountains. You will need all your wits to get there."

"The Serpent Mountains!" whispered George nervously. "They sound really scary."

"And dangerous," added Pedro.

"A gang of big strong Anagranimals like you don't have anything to be worried about," said the Wishing Tree encouragingly, "I'm sure you'll be just fine."

The gang looked unconvinced.

"That's easy for you to say," said George, "you don't have a juicy duck's bottom. What if we get eaten by a hungry lion?"

"Lions don't eat ducks," snapped Lancelot, "they're far too bony,"

"No. But they might take a bite out of a Pig-Orilla-Roo," offered Rocky mischievously.

"Ok. I tell you what," sighed the Wishing Tree, "I shall teach you a magic spell that will let you swap animal parts between yourselves. By swapping body parts and using different combinations you will be able to do almost anything. Then there really won't be anything to be scared of."

"I suppose that would be helpful," said George, sounding a little less afraid.

"And quite a lot of fun," added Pedro. "How does the magic spell work?"

"All you need to do is hold hands with the friend you want to swap with," explained the Wishing Tree. "Then close your eyes, think about the body part that you want to change and say the magic words,

"Higgledy biggledy boo,
let's swap body parts me and you."

The gang took turns at practising the magic spell. Heidi and Pedro went first. They stood close, held hands and whispered the magic words together.

"Higgledy biggledy boo, let's swap body parts me and you."

"Poof". No sooner had the magic words been spoken than there was a puff of purple smoke.

"Look. It worked!!!" spluttered George holding his nose and flapping the smoke away with his wings.

As if by magic, Heidi and Pedro had swapped body parts. Heidi had been transformed into a Hippo-Rilla-Roo with big bulging gorilla muscles and a huge pair of kangaroo feet whilst Pedro had become a Piggy-Croco-Puss with Heidi's crocodile body and her pussy cat paws.

"Hee hee!" giggled Rocky watching on. "This is going to be a hoot! We should get going. We've got a Weeping Willow to find!" And with that the gang set off on their first adventure.

To read the story of the Anagranimals and the Weeping Willow and all the other Anagranimal stories go to www.Anagranimals.com.

www.Anagranimals.com